CELIO'S MOUNTAIN

.... a place to dream

Joy N Perkins

Balboa Press books may be ordered through booksellers or by contacting:

Balboa Press
A Division of Hay House
1663 Liberty Drive
Bloomington, IN 47403
www.balboapress.com.au
1 (877) 407-4847

ISBN: 978-1-5043-1526-5 (sc)
ISBN: 978-1-5043-1527-2 (e)

Print information available on the last page.

Balboa Press rev. date: 11/13/2018

BALBOA.
PRESS
A DIVISION OF HAY HOUSE

Author's Dedication:

This book is dedicated to my brother Kevin Charles Perkins. For all that he was and everything he strived for. He will be my forever hero, my voice of reason and the man who did things his way, always.

I love you.

Joy

CELIO'S MOUNTAIN

.... a place to dream.

Written: Joy N Perkins

Illustrated: Shawn Westwood

Puddletown Lane

High on the mountains very close to the Sacred Valley of Machu Picchu, is the village of Pampa.

In the village is a little hut and a family sits around the heat of the fire.

They are awaiting the arrival of their newest family member.

They are *very* excited.

They know their Mama Maria, is working hard.

They pray for her health and for the safe arrival of the new baby.

Then they hear the welcome call, "Come quickly", says Papi.
"Come and see your new little brother." He is very proud.

"Mama Maria and I, will name him Celio", he smiled.
Everyone was very happy and together they looked into the new baby's crib.
"What a beautiful little boy, he is", said big sister Sara.

The family sat quietly and watched while Celio slept in his mother's arms.

"Ssh", says Papi "Can you hear the lullaby Mama is singing to your little brother".

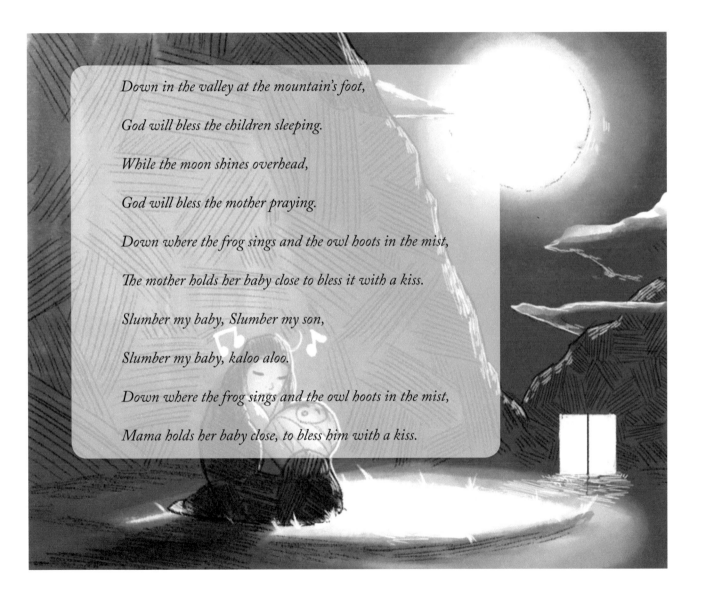

Down in the valley at the mountain's foot,

God will bless the children sleeping.

While the moon shines overhead,

God will bless the mother praying.

Down where the frog sings and the owl hoots in the mist,

The mother holds her baby close to bless it with a kiss.

Slumber my baby, Slumber my son,

Slumber my baby, kaloo aloo.

Down where the frog sings and the owl hoots in the mist,

Mama holds her baby close, to bless him with a kiss.

Celio began to grow and was a very happy little boy.

He loved to play peekaboo with his brothers and sisters.

"Peekaboo, Celio", they giggled at their little brother. "Peekaboo".

"Kaboo", laughed Celio. "Kaboo".

And while his mama was in the kitchen, cooking food, he
listened to her singing as she worked.

"Down where the frogs sing and the owl hoots in the mist,
The mother holds her baby close to bless it with a kiss."

Celio loved to eat his mama's cooking.

"Oh goodness, Celio", laughed Mama. "You do love your dinner, don't you?"

"You will grow strong, very soon, my son," she said.

Celio smiled his brightest smile.

So it was not long before Celio was running and playing in the fields, while Papi Luis and his brothers worked to bring in the corn.

"Well done, Celio," said Papi. "That's right, put it in the basket". Celio smiled. He liked to work hard and this pleased his father. He took the big cobs of corn and while it was tough work for a little boy, he managed to fill the baskets every day.

Celio was always excited when the harvest was complete, because his brothers taught him to play soccer. He ran and laughed and learned to kick. "Yes, Celio, that is good", shouted his brothers, as they ran through the corn stalks. "That is excellent," they laughed, watching him kick the ball high into the air.
They taught him to slide…..

They taught him to head the ball.

They taught him how to jump the ball

But, most of all, they loved to teach him special tricks.

Celio's strength grew and so did his capacity to work.

But one day, he noticed that his brothers were not smiling.

In fact, they did not go out into the fields to play after finishing the day's work.

"Is there something wrong, Roli?" Celio asked. "You do not laugh today."

His big brother put his arm around his shoulder.

"We must go home now," he said. "Mama is waiting for us."

On their way back to the village, Celio saw something different in the streets. Instead of the happy, hustle and bustle, people were standing in long lines. The markets had closed and the usual music was replaced by silence.

When he stopped and stared, Roli took his arm and pulled him aside. He whispered, "We need to go now and when we are home, we will learn more."

Inside their home, Mama Maria and Papi Luis sat everyone down, then he cleared his throat, "Hmmm, hmm!" He looked around at all the solemn faces and said in a low voice, "We have come to learn that there will be changes to our way of life," Everyone leaned in closer to hear what Papi had to say.

"This means we must work very hard to keep each other safe."

Then he looked at Celio and said, "All the schools will close for a while and for now we must work and that means no games. I need to put your soccer ball away."

Celio was sad, but before he could object, Papi Luis said kindly, "You will be sad for a while son, but we are good people and we will work hard and care for one another."

Celio moved closer to his mother and sat with her by the fire. He said, "You know I am a strong boy, so I will be a good helper for everyone in our home."

His family smiled and his big brother Denis roughed his hair.

Mama laughed and said, "I know Celio. You are a good boy. We look forward to happier days."

That night, as Celio lay in his bed, he could hear his parents talking and the clinking of the pots on the stove. When his mother began to sing – he finally drifted off to sleep.

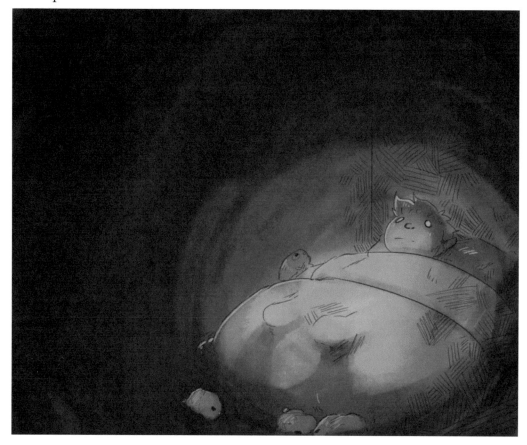

Down in the valley at the mountain's foot –

God will bless the children sleeping,

While the moon's high overhead,

God will bless the mother praying.

The very next day, Celio walked to the village market to wait in line, holding a shopping bag, with a few coins to buy grain for the evening meal.
He looked across at the snow-covered peaks of the mountain range.

While he was sad he could not go to school or play soccer, he knew in his heart everything would work out alright for his family.
He watched the mist over the mountain and the low-lying clouds gave him comfort.

Then, through this wondrous sky-scape, a mighty condor swooped and dipped and cut through the fluffy whiteness and hovered momentarily, while it looked down below onto the streets.

It was as though he was searching for something. Then he circled slowly, slowly, his bright eyes darting back and forth as he scanned the crowd.

Celio was sure the condor was looking for him.

He whistled softly to himself, then declared, "Oh my, you are a beautiful bird!" Then he smiled broadly and added, "I will name you, Alejandro." From then on, every day, Celio looked to the sky for his new friend.

That evening, while Celio sat by the fire with his Mama, he said,
"I was looking at the mountains today and they seem to me, to be very strong."

Mama laughed. "Yes, Celio – the mountains are very strong." She thought a moment, then added,
"Every rock and crevice, every trail and tree is an important part of the Sacred
Valley. It is the home of the Inca kings and the legacy they have left is a reminder
for us to uphold the memory of our ancestors."
He nodded, thoughtfully and his mama continued, "The Inca people came here to
Peru a long time ago, and built the city at Machu Picchu and all of the terraces
you now see, all around our country."

Celio pulled himself closer to his mother. She smiled, "Their city in the Sacred Valley is a continual reminder of how intelligent, wise and strong, their nation was." "Of course," said Celio. "But why did they build their city so high. It's as though they wanted to be sure no one would find it."

Mama said, "Maybe it was because they wanted to be closer to their gods."

Celio smiled and came closer still. She thought for a moment and added, "Maybe they wanted to be high enough so they could hear what their gods were saying, up above the clouds," and she smiled at Celio's wide eyes.

Celio smiled too, then he nodded and yawned. It was time for bed.

"May we talk some more about the mountains; and the Sacred Valley; and the Sun Gate; and the great Inca nation; and the, the, the, the...", his voiced trailed off.

"Yes, of course", Mama said. "Tomorrow night, I promise."

Mama led Celio to his bed and while his eyes were closing, she blew out the candle and began to sing,

> *Down where the frog sings and the owl hoots in the mist,*
> *The mother holds her baby close to bless it with a kiss.*

"Goodnight, Celio," she whispered, "sleep well, my son."

In his sleep, Celio dreamed of the gods in the mists, over the mountains in Machu Picchu. He saw the great kings in their robes, wearing silver crowns, uplifting their spears to the sky.

He saw the swirling clouds and the condors swooping and flying overhead.

Then he heard someone calling his name. "Celio, Celio."

He knew it was the voice of the 'gods'... He held his breath.

Then, suddenly ... he was awake.

It was his big brother Denis, smiling down at him.

"Come on, wake up!"

Celio grumbled. He wanted to go back to sleep so he could talk to the Inca kings.
He wanted to speak to the their gods. But Denis pulled him out from under the
covers and helped him get dressed.

While the family ate their morning meal, Celio asked, "Mama, will you
take me up to the city in the Sacred Valley, one day?"

He said, "I would like to go high enough so that I can talk with the gods like the Inca people did." Mama smiled kindly and nodded. His brothers and sisters looked at each other. They knew Celio loved to learn and said, "Celio, when you come back this evening, we will continue with our tales of the Sacred Valley and our land of Peru".

It was still very early when he left the family home, and while Celio was waiting for his friends, he looked far beyond the mountains and imagined being high enough to feel the crisp air on his face and feel the wind in his hair.

He could hear the faint call of the condors as they flew way across the valley. Deep inside his heart, he could sense the stirring of a hope that one day, he would be able to learn more of the history of his homeland. He couldn't wait to talk with his mother again.

That evening, he began to ask more questions. He'd been planning all day.

Waiting for the right moment, he blurted out, "Mama, please tell me more about the city of Machu Picchu."

Mama smiled, she was proud her son wanted to learn. "The city nestles by the Urubamba River, Celio. American archeologist, Hiram Bingham III discovered it in 1911, with the help of local guides. They followed an ancient Inca trail and when they got to the spot they call The Sun Gate, they looked down over the ruins which have now been restored."

Celio looked at his mother in surprise. She laughed and continued. "It is believed that the city was built for the Inca Emperor and his family.

Because it was so isolated, the solitude was perfect for worship in the Temple of the Sun. The Inca priests and astronomers studied the stars in the reflection of the water pools in the observatories."

Celio was fascinated. "Oh how I would have loved to have been there with him to see the city for the first time," Celio laughed. He tried to imagine standing beside the explorer and discovering the city of the Incas for the first time.

"Mama where can I learn more about the history of my homeland?" Celio asked.

"At school," Mama said. "There is coming a time when you will be able to go back and learn your lessons," she added. "All of the colleges and the universities are opening again very soon," she said with a smile.

Celio liked this idea, very much. He looked at his mother with a twinkle in his eye and said, "Maybe then, I could be an instructor, or an explorer and I could speak to people who come to my country and tell them all about the Sacred Valley." Mama laughed, "Of course, Celio. If you work hard enough you can achieve many things," she smiled. "Who knows, maybe, one day you will be able to hear the voices of the Inca gods up on the mountain in Machu Picchu."

In bed that night, Celio closed his eyes and smiled to himself. He would do something that would keep the history of his ancestors alive. He wanted to help others and he knew now, more than anything, that studying to be a teacher, would be the best way he could achieve his goal.

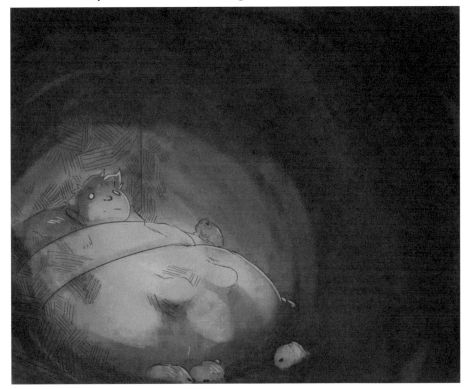

He thought about his mama's words: "If you work hard you can achieve many things." Slipping gently into sleep, he 'saw' himself on the mountain, surrounded by his eager students, listening to every word he said. "What a lovely day that will be!" thought Celio, as he drifted off into slumber.

So the years passed and Celio grew to be a young man.

There were changes in his country and just as his mama promised, he was able to go back to school.

He learned his lessons well and went on to University to study.

Then one day he was asked if he would assist with a group of new international students, who were keen to learn about local history. Celio was very pleased to be of help. "Of course, I would be delighted," he said.

They set off on the bus and when they arrived at the Sacred Valley, a storm was coming in from the south. Celio led his students up the steep paths and stairways, describing how the early Incans had created the terraces. The wind was picking up and the clouds were starting to roll in. However, he used the rough weather as an example of the hardships these people must have experienced back in the 1400's, when setting out the plans for the city. He pointed out the way in which the mighty slabs of granite had been placed with intricate precision and watched the amazement on the faces of his students.

When Celio reached the highest point, he turned and looked out over the Sacred Valley and down onto the city. The black cloud-banks were low in the sky and even as the lightning flashed, the sun found a tiny space and broke through, sending shafts of bright light across the valley. One of the students shouted, "Oh, look! A condor – isn't it magnificent!"

Celio turned his eyes upward and watched as the mighty creature swooped and dipped through the thick white clouds. The rain on its feathers sprayed outward catching the sunlight creating a burst of rainbow colors. With its wings stretched wide and proud, it rose on an updraft and plunged swiftly toward the small group of students below.

Celio knew this was no coincidence and even before he felt the spray wash over him while the bird flew past, he whispered, "Alejandro, is that you? How is it possible that you would find me here, my old friend?"

The deep understanding and full realization of the journey he had been on, came in a rush of joyous emotion. He recalled his mother's voice, "If you work hard Celio, you will achieve many things." All of the struggles he had gone through in his life, were lessons that had directed his feet to these terraces. He was where his ancestors had once stood and in his own way, he would continue to enrich the journey and the lives of others as he guided them on his history tours. Despite the storm, the laughter of his students, made him smile. They looked out over the Sacred Valley with that special thrill of excitement and delight that comes when discovering something for the very first time.

Taking in the scene before him, Celio watched as the storm raged. Tourists from all over the world were running to the bus shelters and the keepers were taking the alpacas and their babies from off the terraces, to put them into their pens before nightfall. The thunder roared and bolts of lightning ripped through the sky in a dramatic display of power.

Celio thought he could hear the voices of the Inca gods, so he closed his eyes and listened. He imagined Pachucutec, the last Emperor of the Incas, calling his name - "Celio…. Celio. Welcome to our mountain. Welcome to the Sacred Valley".

His Mama had been right all along.

He had worked hard and in this moment, he knew he had achieved his dream.

....este no es el final!

For Celio ….

Let my dreams be bigger than my fears –
And my actions louder than my words.

Chi Miigwech!

Glossary:

Find these words – they are hidden in the book.

Capacity – ability, skill

Solemn – serious

Nestles – lies comfortably

Isolated – away from everything

Solitude – aloneness

Intricate – careful

Precision – accurate

Observatories – places to study the stars

Printed in the United States
By Bookmasters